KU-229-958

Silly Poems

Warning

If poetry that's sensible
Is what you're searching for
If you want words of wisdom
Then you need search no more

For this is not the book for you
So do not waste your money
This book is full of silly stuff
And poems that are funny!

Celia Stanzas

Other fantastic poetry
collections from Scholastic:

Disgusting Poems
Magic Poems
Animal Poems
Family Poems
Pet Poems
School Poems
Spooky Poems
Funny Poems

Silly Poems

Compiled by
Paul Cookson

Illustrated by
Sarah Nayler

For Paul, Bev, Isabel and Edward

First published in the UK by The Book People Ltd in 2005
Hall Wood Avenue, Haydock, St Helens WA11 9UL UK

This collection copyright © Paul Cookson, 2005
Illustrations copyright © Sarah Nayler, 2005

Copyright information for individual poems is given on page 114, which
constitutes an extension of this copyright page.

10 digit ISBN 0 439 95053 8
13 digit ISBN 978 0439 95053 4

All rights reserved

Printed and bound by Nørhaven Paperback A/S, Denmark

1 2 3 4 5 6 7 8 9 10

This book is sold subject to the condition that it shall not, by way of trade
or otherwise, be lent, resold, hired out, or otherwise circulated without
the publisher's prior consent in any form of binding or cover other
than that in which it is published and without a similar condition,
including this condition, being imposed upon the subsequent purchaser.

Papers used are made from wood grown in sustainable forests

CONTENTS

Nursery Rhymes and Silly Stories

Loopy Limericks

Puny Puns and Wacky Wordplay

Nutty Nonsense

Last Word

Acknowledgements

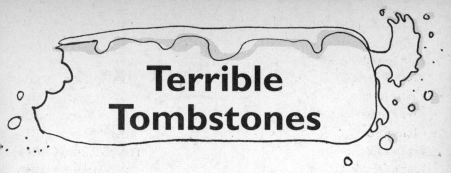

Terrible Tombstones

Beneath these pages and these headstones
Lie epitaphs and tombstone poems

The jokes are awful, the puns half formed
Grave humour ahead – you have been warned!

Edward Stones

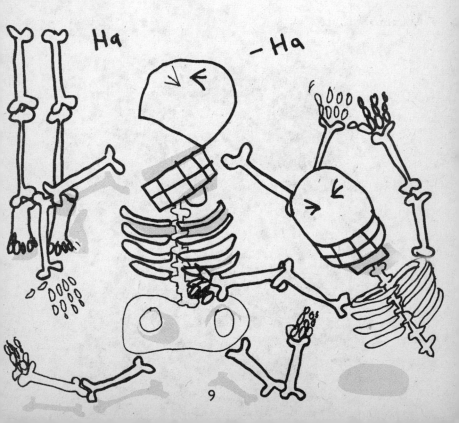

Spud-u-will-not-like

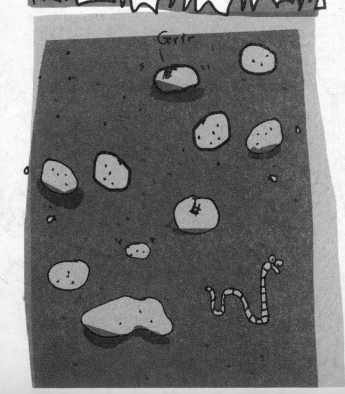

Here lie bad potatoes
Neither mashed nor boiled
Rejects – six feet under –
Definitely soiled

Stewart Henderson

King Harold

Beneath this stone
Here I lie.
I got something
In my eye.

Peter Dixon

A Slimline Grave

A dietician lies
Beneath this slab.
(Just skin and bones –
No fat or flab!)

He dieted for YEARS –
So it's ironic that
The maggots and worms
Are now growing FAT!

Trevor Harvey - .

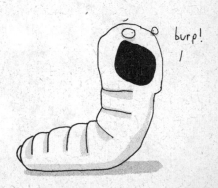

burp!

Death of a Dog Burglar

When he broke in the Rottweiler kennels one night
He wasn't expecting to die
But the teeth in the dark were monstrous and sharp
He should have let sleeping dogs lie.

Paul Cookson

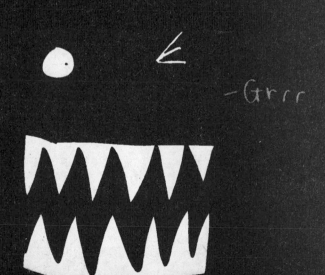

What a Way to Go!

Poor Jed
Died in bed
From a boil upon his head.

Felicity
Played with electricity
O Benedicite!

Poor Solly
Died from not
cooking propolly!
E. Coli.

Poor Kelly
Died from a leak in her left welly
Very smelly.

Poor Ali
Was very pally
With a snake, intestinally.

Poor Matt,
Felt flat
When a rhino stepped on his hat!

Poor Roly
Our Goalie
Let fifteen in, he *will* die slowly!

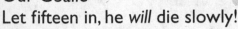

D. Preece
D. Ceased
& D. Creased.

Poor Paul
Died in thrall
To publishers, from reading too many poems,
That's all!

Eric Petrie

Assassination

Here lies my Barbie doll –
Pretty, pink and dead.
My horrid little brother
Has just blown off her head.

Karen Costello-McFeat

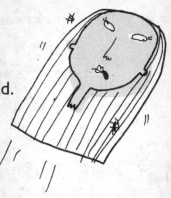

A Grave Mistake

This grave was never meant for you
It was for Lucky Jim
It's strange that Jim is still alive
It's strange that you fell in

Daniel Lawrence Phelps

Epitaph

Here lies a man who chewed his nails,
and when he'd eaten those,
he tucked into his other parts.
Or so the story goes.

He made a start on both his feet,
ate ankles, soles and toes;
he gobbled up each leg and limb
and then, so we suppose,

he worked his way up to the top
from bottom up to beard,
and then, poor man, he had to stop,
because he'd disappeared.

David Horner

Fame

He lived his life untouched by fame,
and when he died it was the same,
for in this grave lies –

"What's his name?"

Brian G D'Arcy

Epitaph for the Last Martian

Crash landing caused extinction
For the last of the Martian species
Here and here … and here and here
He rests in pieces

Paul Cookson

Miles' Stone

This tombstone is a milestone.
Ha! How so?
Because beneath lies Miles, who's
Miles below.

Anon

Ridiculous Riddles

Riddle Me Wrong

My first is in scare but not in fright
My second in spooky, no that's not right
My third is in riddle but not in ree
My fourth's in the fog and I'm all at sea
I can't find my fifth, just lost my first
Of all the puzzles, this seems the worst
I'll make a new start, a brand new riddle
Lose the whole thread, get stuck in the middle
My first has gone bonkers, my second's gone west
Forget the whole business, that'll be best.

David Harmer

Animal Quiz (v. difficult)

Why is the Ost rich?
How did the Hippo pot a mouse?

When does the Oka pee?
Why should the Walla be?

What turns a Pyth on?
What does the Sea lie on?

With whom did the Ant elope?
And when did the Boa constrict her?

What makes the Butter fly, the Ham stir?
Just how much can a Grizzly Bear?

What if it should Rain, dear?
What if it should Rain deer?

Trevor Parsons

23

Riddle-me-ree

Here's a riddle you'll really love,
One that's quite inspired –
How did the cannonball lose its job?
The poor old thing was fired...

Cool

Yeah

Now here's a riddle to make you guess,
You'll never get it right –
What's very, very noisy
And coloured black and white?

You see, you didn't know it,
So here the answer comes –
A music-mad young zebra
With a brand-new set of drums...

The STRIPES

Now riddles get dafter and dafter,
Take the one that I heard yesterday –
The electrician was late getting home,
So what did his angry wife say?

Come on then, just fasten your seatbelt,
'Cos this one you're sure going to hate –
What did she say to her hubby?
"Wire you insulate…?"

Now here's a riddle to make you smile,
Perhaps you'll even laugh –
What do you get if you cross a dog
With an extra tall giraffe?

The answer's simple really,
Although perhaps inane –
You get an animal that barks
At every low-flying plane…

Clive Webster

Mapping It Out
(A Perplexing Puzzle)

Ten cyclists in the USA
Took turns to ride on a bike each day,
Back and forth, from State to State.
(While one was riding, the rest would wait.)
Each, in turn, would spend a day
Pedalling furiously and make their way
To another State, where they would find
The next one waiting – then stay behind
While the new one journeyed to a *different* State,
Where *another* cyclist had been told to wait.

And, for this trip, each had a map
To make sure there was NO mishap.

Each travelled just as had been planned.
They rode from Maine to Maryland,
North Dakota, Idaho,
Oklahoma, New Mexico,
Indiana and Oregon,
Alabama and Washington.

And then, as if to make things worse,
Each did their *day's trip* in reverse!

Washington and Alabama,
Oregon and Indiana,
New Mexico and Oklahoma,
Idaho and North Dakota,
Maryland and Maine.
Till each was safely home again,
Back in the State where they had started.

So, in what State was their CYCLE,
When they parted...?

Answer:

Worn out!

Trevor Harvey

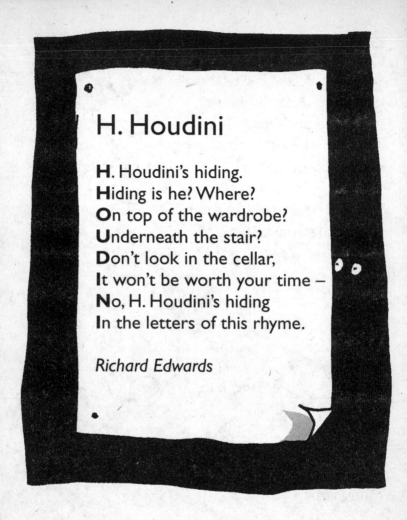

H. Houdini

H. Houdini's hiding.
Hiding is he? Where?
On top of the wardrobe?
Underneath the stair?
Don't look in the cellar,
It won't be worth your time –
No, H. Houdini's hiding
In the letters of this rhyme.

Richard Edwards

Shortest Riddle In The World

Zip ....

Splat!

What am I?

(A fly banging into a window)

Matt Black

Fighting Fit

(A crazy puzzle poem for you to complete with the following words: mad, sad, bad, dad, lad, fad, rad, glad.)

Was a glad iator a happy fighter?
Was a __ iator an evil blighter?

Did a __ iator combat the chill?
Was a __ iator over the hill?

Did a __ iator fight back the tears?
Was a __ iator lacking in years?

Was a __ iator the champ in favour?
Was a __ iator a rant and raver?

Philip Waddell

Naughty Acrostic

Know what type of poem I am? I am an acrosti**C**
Never, you say. Not a proper one. Oh yes says **I**
If you study me so very closely you will see tha**T**
Clearly, the letters at the end of each of the line**S**
Kindly fit together if you look at the columns t**O**
Easily form a word for the benefit of the reade**R**
Rude! No … upside down, back to front, ad ho**C**
See what I mean! I am an acrostic after all … ah**A**

Paul Cookson

What's In My Basket?

There's something in my shopping basket.
You'll never guess what.
You'll never guess what.
OK.
While I'm in the queue
I'll give you a clue.

It's used for cleaning.
— Two words —
First one meaning
"Wet marshy ground"
Any idea yet?
Any idea yet?
It's something we all need
Has soft sheets
Spins round
Readily at hand
Any idea yet?
Any idea yet?

Second word
Sounds like "coal", "bowl",
"stole" and "scroll"
But means "to turn over and over".
Any idea yet?
Any idea yet?

It comes in colours white, pink,
Yellow, peach and blue.
Any idea yet?
Any idea yet?

No?
Answer's upside down, below:

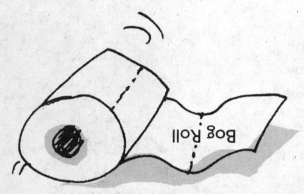

Ian Corns

Loopy Lists

Ten Rhyming Things That Should Not Be Eaten

Railway trains
Snow chains
Bottled brains
Blocked drains
Aeroplanes
Water mains
Window panes
Horses' reins
Archaeological remains

As they will give you
Stomach pains

John Coldwell

A Batty Booklist

Highway Robbery by Stan Dan Deliver

Cheap Ornaments by Nick Nacks

Fortune Telling by Crystal Ball

Bad Hair Days by Dan Druff

Ups and Downs by C Saw and Ellie Vator

Keep Fit by Jim Nastics

Mouthwatering Foods by Sally Vate

Traffic Dodging by J Walker

Make It Snappy! by Allie Gator

The Ass's Tale by Don Key

Winner Takes All by Jack Pot

Utter Nonsense by Tommy Rot

John Foster

An Alphabet Of Alphabeastical Facts You Didn't Know You Knew

Ants cannot play tubas
Bats cannot hit balls
Crocodiles can't rock and roll
Dolphins can't climb walls

Emus can't do DIY
Flies can't ride a bike
Gnus can't read the news
Horses cannot write

Iguanas cannot rollerskate
Jackdaws can't play guitars
Kangaroos can't conga
Llamas can't drive cars

Monkeys can't do crosswords
Newts can't play trombones
Orang-utans can't deep-sea dive
Penguins can't use telephones

Quala Bears can't spell
Rhinos cannot tightrope walk
Squids cannot climb trees
Tarantulas can't squawk

Unicorns can't belly dance
Vipers cannot ski
Wombats cannot surf the net
Xtinct things can't be

Yetis can't be spotted
Zebras can't turn blue
All these amazing facts
You didn't know you knew

Paul Cookson

Dog's Swear Words

Furballs
Catsbum
It's-too-wet
Catswee
Ratspoo
Bath-time
Vet

Roger Stevens

Never Seen…

Never seen a hyena with a vacuum cleaner,
never seen a goat in a boat.
Never seen a pike on a motorbike
but I've seen an anaconda in a Honda.

Never seen a fish in a satellite dish,
never seen a whale in the Royal Mail.
Never seen a llama unpeel a banana
but I've seen an anaconda in a Honda.

Never seen a tadpole do a forward roll,
never seen a frog weightlifting a log.
Never seen a poodle cooking noodles
but I've seen an anaconda in a Honda.

Never seen a panda in an armoured tank,
never seen a tortoise at a taxi rank.
Never seen a tiger rob a national bank
but I've seen an anaconda in a Honda.

And I've watched him wander and weave

all over the road!

Brian Moses

Christmas Party Invitation List

Greta Warmly
Honor Doorstep
Carol Singer
Belinda Hand
Donna Party-Hat
Paula Cracker
Buster Balloon
Cary Okey
Ava Beveridge
Phil Upwell
Bob About
Dan Surround
Trudy Knight
Tilda Dawn
Mary Christmas

Philip Waddell

Jumble Sale Offer

Here's a sack of –
Single, shapeless, shabby, smelly,
Stringy, saggy, short 'n' sporty,
Scruffy, sweaty, scratchy, scabby,
Shoddy, sloppy, sickly, shreddy,
Streaky, steamy, spotty, soggy,
Sooty, scummy, sticky, squelchy,
Smutty, shaggy, silly, soppy
– soiled socks.
– NO THANKS!

Redvers Brandling

Ten Tasty Snacks
That Didn't Catch On

Chocolate covered cockroach cakes
Fish and chip smoothies with extra vinegar
Sugar coated conkers and cabbage sauce
Sweaty sock and onion sandwiches
Baked breezeblock with beetroot dip
Fried cowpat and nettle soup
Lumpy gristle and sour milk biscuits
Liquorice, lemon and lard flavoured crisps
Frozen slugs with snail and spider sauce
Skunk flavoured nibbles with toenail nachos

David Harmer

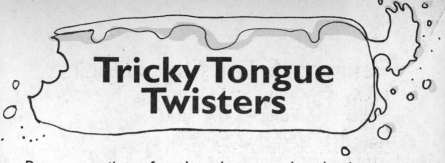

Tricky Tongue Twisters

Repeat until confused, embarrassed or both

He felt smart
She felt smart
They both felt smart together

He felt smart
She felt smart
They both felt smart together

Anon

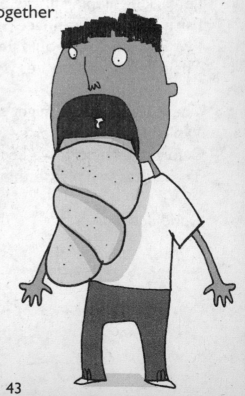

Flicking Off The Filthy Flecks

I'm flicking off these filthy flecks
These fleas leave on my fleece.
I wish these flipping filthy fleas
Would leave my fleece in peace.

But still these fleas leave flecks with ease
And make my fleece a mess,
While if the fleas had fled I'd need
To flick these flecks far less.

I'm flicking flipping flocks of flecks:
Far more than I can face.
I wish these fleas would flee, and leave
Their flecks some other place.

These flipping fleas might spread disease,
Which isn't neat or nice.
Before they next leave flecks, I wish
These fleas will please think twice.

David Bateman

Told You So

Poem to read before you begin searching for those "Summer bargains"

fa   ce

fac   ts

cheap   choice

pink   strap

q u a y s i d e

s e a - s i d e

s h o e   s h o p

s l o p   s l a p

f l i p - f l o p s

s   p
  o o n   s n a

Mike Johnson

Zooming Zoe

Zooming Zoe zig-zags zebras

Round zooming zebras zooming Zoe zig-zags

Zig-zags Zoe zig-zags zooming zebras

Is what zooming Zoe does

Zoe and Jake, aged 11
North Border Junior School

Wigwise

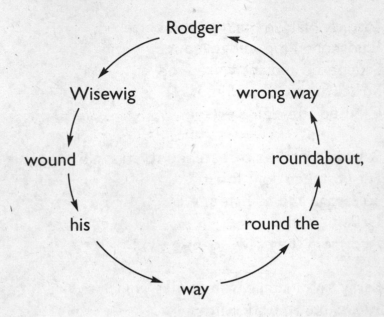

Rodger
Wisewig   wrong way
wound   roundabout,
his   round the
way

Gina Douthwaite

Battling Natalie

Latterly Natalie's belted and battered,
Bludgeoned me, cudgelled me,
Scuppered and splattered me,
Struck at me, butted me,
Clouted and clattered me.

Battling Natalie's threatened to strangle me,
Set both her dogs loose
To savage and mangle me,
Grip me and rip me
And, from their jaws, dangle me.

Barry says Natalie, sometimes, is nice to me,
Wants me to notice her,
Wants some advice from me.
I think she's planning
To cut off a slice of me.

In my dreams, Natalie's ready to slaughter me,
Take my whole body
And bit by bit alter me,
Buffet and blitz me
And hang, draw and quarter me.

Natalie wants me boiled like bacon,
Hung by my toenails
Until I'm mistaken
For bits left behind
From what vultures have taken.

Barry says when she's not there that I've missed her,
That Natalie's fine,
I just need to resist her.
It's easy for him:
She isn't his sister.

David Kitchen

Twong Tister

Try saying "Six slim slender saplings",
"A proper copper coffee pot",
"A truly rural ruler's mural —"
You'll go crackers, like as not.

Say "Sonia shouldn't shun some sunshine",
"That bloke's back brake-block just broke",
"Whistle for the thistle sifter —"
You'll find this vocal test's no joke.

Say "Knapsack strap", "Mixed biscuits",
Say "Crystallized crushed conkers".
On second thoughts, say nowt at all —
You'll end up going bonkers…!

Clive Webster

Naughty Nicole's Knickers

Naughty Nicole nicks naughty knickers at night
At night naughty Nicole naughty knickers nicks
Nicking naughty knickers is what naughty Nicole does
Naughty Nicole is a night-time knicker nicker!

Nicole and Chloe, aged 11
North Border Junior School

Peter Piper
(Easy Version)

Peter Piper chose a large number
Of peppers that had been soaked in vinegar and
spices

A large number of peppers
That had been soaked in vinegar and spices
Was chosen by Peter Piper

If it is indeed true
That Peter Piper chose a large number
Of peppers that had been soaked in vinegar and
spices

Where are they?

Roger Stevens

Jolly Jake

Jolly Jake jumps on jammy dodgers
On jelly jolly jammy dodgers
Jolly Jake Jumps

Zoe and Jake, aged 11
North Border Junior School

Shirley Smithson
(The Stunning Supermarket
Shelf Stacker)

She's a super shelf stacker
Stacking supermarket shelves.
Stacking soups, sorbets and shellfish
Shoppers shouldn't shift themselves.

She's so stylish, simply stunning,
Startled shoppers stop in shock.
Standing stocking, never stopping,
Shining shelves supplied with stock.

Ian Larmont

Happy Haikus and Crazy Clerihews

Haiku or High Queue?

It's when pigeons say
hello to each other "Hi
coo-hi-coo hi-coo"

Or folks lining up
waiting for the lift on the
twenty-second floor.

Paul Cookson

Superman

Superman
helps people whenever he can
and deals with miscreants
by frightening them in his underpants.

Jill Townsend

Flu Haiku

Sometimes your nose feels
like it's full of cotton wool
even when it's snot.

Clare Kirwan

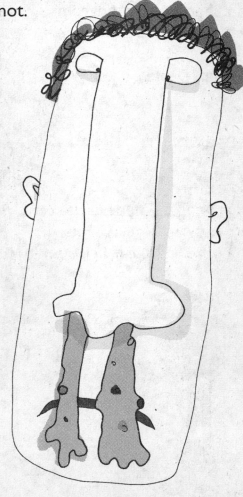

Men in Tights

While Robin Hood
looked rather good,
the Sheriff of Nottingham
was not quite so hot in 'em.

Graham Denton

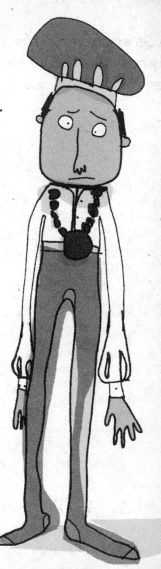

IQ Haiku

IQs are made from
three lions of five, seven
and five silly bulls.

Trevor Parsons

Four Soccer Clerihews

Said David Beckham,
"Goal nets? I wreck 'em"
And he does frequently beat defenders
With his famous free kick benders.

I can really enthuse
About Sir Stanley Matthews:
He was the Wizard of Dribble.
About that there can be no quibble.

They said Michael Owen
Would soon be goin'
To Real Madrid.
And in the end he did.

Zinedine Zidane
Most certainly can
With a brilliant pass turn a game.
He also has a rather wonderful name.

Eric Finney

The Rapping Haiku

The rapping haiku
Has a beat. The audience
Start to tap their feet.

Rapping haikus are
Really neat. They make you want
To dance down the street.

So click your fingers.
Give a clap. Let's all do the
Rapping haiku rap.

John Foster

Peter Pan

Peter Pan
Drove a van
Over Wendy
Now she's bendy

Andrea Shavick

Nursery Rhymes and Silly Stories

Hey Diddle Diddle

Hey diddle diddle
The cat and the fiddle
The cow jumped over the bed
The little dog laughed
But not for long
'Cos the cow landed right on his head.

Roger Stevens

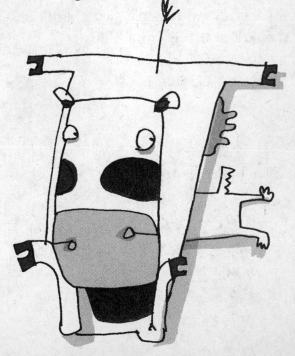

Hurly-Burly Early Rhymes

Mary, Mary, quite contrary:
She's grown a beard.
Very scary!

Little Bo Peep has lost her sheep,
And doesn't know where to find them.
If she'd only put her glasses on,
She'd know she was just behind them.

Baa, Baa, Black Sheep,
Have you any wool?
Of course I haven't, silly child!
Can't you see I'm a bull?

Trevor Dickinson

Three Little Dogs

This little dog went to Margate,
This little dog stayed at Rome,
And this little dog had a wee-wee-wee
On a lamp-post near his home.

Tim Hopkins

Jack

Peter Dixon

First Lines of Long Lost Nursery Rhymes

Humpty Dumpty sat on a gate
Humpty Dumpty leant on the fence
Humpty Dumpty sat on a cat
Little Jack Horner was sick in the corner
Little Jack Lance got stuck in his pants
Little Miss Cider sat on a spider
Little Miss Moylet sat on the toilet
The Grand Old Duke Of York
He had ten thousand pairs of underpants

Paul Cookson

Why You Should Never Play On Roads

There was a boy called Lawrence Lowdes
Who liked to play on busy roads.

To make his pulse and heart rate quicken
He would play a game of chicken.

At the very last moment out he'd race
Laughing in the driver's face.

He scampered out in front of bikes
Buses, scooters, vans and trikes,

Cars and lorries, four-wheeled drives
Like a cat with ninety lives.

Lawrence felt so bored one day
He thought he'd try a motorway.

Things move there at greater speed
Giving Lol the thrill he'd need.

Soon his interest was caught
By a giant juggernaut.

Lawrence got himself prepared
And waiting longer than he dared

Out he ran, laughed and tripped
And by those massive tyres was gripped.

Round he whirled stuck to each wheel
But nobody could hear him squeal.

The moral is as clear as that
Little Lawrence was squashed flat.

So now across the nation's roads
Are lorry loads of Laurie Lowdes.

David Harmer

The Cautionary Tale Of Annabelle Thaw

Annabelle Agnes Angelica Thaw
dreamt only of being a dinosaur.

Night and day she pored studiously over a book
to learn when to bellow and how she should
  look…

Her brother declared as she practised her roar
that Annabelle Agnes was now quite a bore.

Her parents decided they'd try to ignore
the fact that their dear daughter's hand was a claw.

Her mother tried cooking her favourite meal
but Annabelle Agnes let out a huge squeal:

"I can't eat that meat, it's not even raw –
and besides, can't you see I'm a young
  HERBIVORE?"

In despair they served grass-cuttings piled on her
  plate …
then watched in dismay as the herbivore ate.

"We wanted a girl, not a great dinosaur!"
but their favourite rose disappeared down her jaw.

Her father, who'd not met this problem before,
stroked his beard and suggested consulting the law.

But Annabelle Agnes continued to gnaw
till the garden had gone — and she still wanted
   more!

Now the garden was bare she ate tables, a chair;
she chewed mattresses, carpets and sofas — a pair!

She gulped clothes pegs and pillows — the
   neighbours all puzzled
at how she digested the gunk that she guzzled.

But Annabelle Agnes, devouring a drawer,
asked what they could offer a starved dinosaur.

Her father said grimly, "This has to be war!"
but the herbivore just couldn't squeeze through
   the door;

One footstep alone pinned her gran to the floor.
(Her grandpa, quite shocked, cried, "That looks
rather sore!")

There was no turning back now for Annabelle
   Thaw
till one day she was traced ...
   by a huge CARNIVORE!

That day, as young Annabelle chewed through a flex
She was eaten herself … by a ravenous T-rex!

Judith Nicholls

New Rhymes For Old

Jack Sedge would eat no veg.
His wife would eat no meats;
and so between them both, you see,
they lived on cakes and sweets.

Hickory, dickory, dock!
The mouse ran down my sock.
The sock did pong,
the mouse was gone.
Hickory, dickory, dock!

Jack be nimble,
Jack be quick,
Jack jump over
the baby's sick.

David Horner

Nursery

My mum says
once I came home from nursery
with a sulky look on my face.

"What's the matter?" she said.
I said nothing.
"What's the matter?" she said.
I said nothing.
"What's the matter?"
"I had to sit on the naughty chair."

"Why did you have to sit on the naughty chair?"
I said nothing.
"Why did you have to sit on the naughty chair?"
"'Cos I was being naughty."
"Yes yes, I guessed that," she says,
"But what were you doing?"

"I was playing about at singing time,
I wasn't singing the right things."

"What was everyone singing?"
"Baa baa black sheep."
"And what were you singing?"
I said nothing.
"What were you singing?"

"Baa-baa moo-moo."

Michael Rosen

Loopy Limericks

There Was A Young Poet From Limerick

There was a young poet from Limerick
Who was always very confused
'Cos nothing much rhymed
With the town of his birth
So why name a rhyming verse after it?

Paul Cookson

Fred

A stupid young fellow called Fred
Went around with a cat on his head.
I asked, "Why a cat
Do you wear as a hat?"
"'Cos a horse is too heavy," he said.

Barry Buckingham

False Teeth

Owned by a lady called Cottam.
When she smiled she was glad she had got 'em.
They were left on a chair,
She forgot they were there,
And she bit herself right on the bottom.

Ian Larmont

That Dreadful Pupil
From Leicester

There was a young pupil from Leicester
Who would go to her teachers and peicester
She would lock them indoors
Glue their feet to the floors
Till finally they came to arreicester

Trevor Millum

Limerick

The servants of Samuel Pepys
Told neighbours "The man never slepys –
He prowls round the town
Noting everything down
In his diary. It gives us the crepys!"

Sue Cowling

Science Lesson

We've done "Water" and "Metals" and "Plastic",
today it's the turn of "Elastic".
Sir sets up a test…
Wow, that was the best –
he whizzed through the window. Fantastic!

Mike Johnson

There Was A Goalkeeper From Seoul

There was a goalkeeper from Seoul
Who slept all day long on the whole
He spent the game snoring
But kept teams from scoring
By placing his bed in the goal

Richard Caley

The Year in Limericks

No wonder the season's called Spring:
It's all bounce, it's all burst, it's all zing!
So don't tell me it's wrong
If I break into song:
Hey, ding, ding-a-ling, ding-a-ling!

It's a scene quite familiar in Summer:
The kids looking glummer and glummer.
Continuous rain,
Picnic called off again:
Quite frequently Summer's a bummer.

A tree shed two leaves in the Autumn.
A boy standing under it caught 'em.
He cried, "This is fun!
I'll catch every one!"
So the tree dropped the lot just to thwart him.

Mid-Winter: the snowfall is whopping
And you're walking by slipping and slopping.
Soon it's all turned to slush
And it's mish, mash and mush
And your socks and your shoes are all sopping.

Eric Finney

All in a Knight's Work

A dragon most surely delights
In roasting, well done, those he fights
And then snoozing by day
On a soft bed of hay,
For a dragon sleeps day and hunts knights.

Robert Scotellaro

Explosive Tale

There was a volcano called Dot –
once on maps just a minuscule spot.
But, "I'm hungry!" Dot grumbled
as her insides rumbled.
"And what's more, I'm feeling quite hot!"

Judith Nicholls

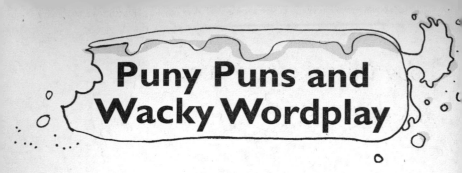

Puny Puns and Wacky Wordplay

The Agnostic Shrimp

Said the big shrimp to the cuttlefish
You may think this odd
I'm a prawn-again crustacean
But I don't believe in cod.

Roger Stevens

Easy Mistake to Make

Andy Seed

Oh, sorry.
You meant write your
Name and address.

Andy Seed

The Total Flop

In sport I'm for the high-jump,
No Fosbury, just a flop.
Got dropped from the karate team.
They've given me the chop.

I go-karted so slowly
That the engine simply rusted.
I tried to throw the discus,
Was so bad I got discusted.

I'm useless on the tennis court
I just can't stand the racket.
I've had it with computer sport,
Given up, can't hack it.

I hurt my neck while batting,
Should've known I'd crick it.
And football's my addiction,
But I wish that I could kick it.

I used to play some snooker
But my game has gone to pot.
Yachting wasn't right for me –
I felt an idi-yacht.

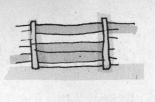

I had a go at fencing
But merely caused a fence.
Tried to lift a hundred pounds
But only raised ten pence.

Hold on though, I think at last
My bad luck's going to stop.
They're hanging out their rugby shirts
And want me for a prop!

Nick Toczek

Please Don't Believe a Word

Your can't wash your hands in a bison;
A hyena has NEVER been tall;
And, whatever Darwin or others might say,
The lynx ISN'T "missing" at all!
A dog that's a boxer won't have a good punch;
A pelican WON'T share the bill;
And do not believe what SOME people have said –
A "sturgeon" WON'T HELP if you're ILL!

Trevor Harvey

Fizz

how
much
fizz
will
fit
into a
bottle?
well, at a
guess, I'd
say quite
a lot'll

James Carter

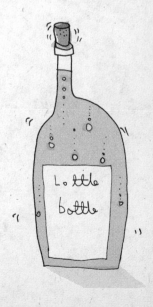

Lottle
bottle

Found Animal Rights Poem

Do not pierce seal

Rupert M Loydell

Sore Sorcerer

To the Wizard's great annoyance
Someone pinched his parking space.
So, after thought, he posted up
A large notice in that place.
In fluorescent colours
The following message showed:

THIS IS THE WIZARD'S PARKING SPACE.
OFFENDERS WILL BE TOAD.

Eric Finney

Itch Hiker

A flea itch-hiked to Paris
as any insect mite.
Most fleas are parasitic,
but he's a Parisite.

Jane Clarke

Bonjour

Octopuzzles

What do you call an octopus with ten legs?
An Octoplus ... Octoplus Two to be exact.

What do you call a medical octopus?
A Doctopus

What do you call an alien octopus with pointed ears?
Spocktopus

What about the electric octopus?
Shocktapus

The night time octopus?
Noctopus

The octopus that likes Chinese cooking?
The Woktopus

An octopus with a dress?
Frocktopus

An octopus that gives the fish rides?
Octobus

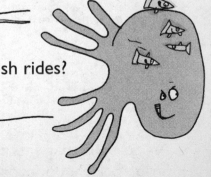

A worried octopus?
Octofuss

A Scottish octopus?
Jocktopus

An octopus with lots of keys?
Locktopus

An octopus that tells the time?
Ticktocktopus

An octopus that wakes you up in the morning?
Alarmclocktopus

An octopus that cleans floors?
Moptopus

An octopus shaped like a brick?
Blocktopus

An octopus made from stone?
Rocktopus

A law enforcement octopus?
Coptopus

An octopus that eats too many Mars Bars?
Choctopus

An octopus that eats too many Rice Krispies?
Snapcrackleandpoptopus

An octopus with woollen feet warmers?
Socktopus

The same octopus, who doesn't wash?
Smellysocktopus

An octopus that always does their homework?
Swottopus

An octopus with one leg?
Hoptopus

An octopus that likes dancing?
Boptopus

The Paul Daniels octopus?
You'regoingtolikethisnotalot-topus

The octopus taken in by another octopus family?
Adoptopus

The octopus whose parents were a crocodile
and a hippo?
Hippocroctopus

The octopus that cannot dive?
Bellyfloptopus

The octopus that you can only see when you join
up numbered points with a pencil?
Dot-to-dot-topus

A dinosaur octopus?
Triceratoptopus

An octopus into martial arts?
Karatechoptopus

An octopus with no legs and no body?
Ed

Enough! I can't take any more
Jokes about the octopus
So make up your own puns
It's time for me to stoptopus

*Paul Cookson and 8MR, North Kesteven School,
North Hykeham*

One Fine Day in the Middle of the Night

One fine day in the middle of the night
Two dead men got up to fight.
Back to back they faced each other,
Drew their swords and shot each other.

Anon

Nutty Nonsense

It's nutty and it's nonsense
Nonsensical and potty
Some of these you'll like a bit
And some you'll like a lotty

Celia Stanzas

Animal Antics

Chimpanzees in dungarees
Do somersaults on the trapeze.

Kangaroos in socks and shoes
Play saxophones and sing the blues.

Elephants in stripy pants
Play basketball with giant ants.

But bumblebees on tiny skis
Struggle to juggle packs of peas.

John Foster

The Man in the Wilderness

The Man in the Wilderness asked of me
"How many blackberries grow in the sea?"
I answered him as I thought good,
"As many red herrings as grow in the wood."

The Man in the Wilderness asked me why
His hen could swim and his pig could fly.
I answered him briskly as I thought best,
"Because they were born in a cuckoo's nest."

The Man in the Wilderness asked me to tell
The sands in the sea and I counted them well.
Says he with a grin, "And not one more?"
I answered him bravely, "You go and make sure!"

Anon

Nonsense II

Myrtle molled the Miller pole
While Tommy twigged the twoo
And Dolly dilled the dripper dole
As Willy wet the woo
Then Andy ate the Acker-cake
And Wendy wonged the groo
As Herbert hacked the matter rake.
And Bertha bonged the boo!
Then all together honged the hack
And widdle donkey doo
They pongled on the wally wall
And the time was half-past two.

Spike Milligan

Frack to Bont

Frack to bont
Tead to hoe
How to sligh
Slick to quow

That to fin
Rare to squound
Quoud to liet
Fost to lound

Nay to dight
Lort to shong
Smig to ball
Streak to wong

Week to mild
Mand to houth
Par to weace
Sorth to nouth

Mun to soon
Gop to sto
Lark to dight
Nes to yo

Frack to bont
Front to back
Opposites always attract

Paul Cookson

Uncle Upside-Down

Meet your Uncle Upside-Down,
a man who's never got his feet on the ground;
pants on my head, socks to my elbows,
at bedtime a pillow's where my backside goes.

Uncle Upside-Down, Uncle Upside-Down,
my manners and appearance are rightly renowned –
shiny shoes on my hands, silk gloves on my toes;
when I've finished on the loo, I always wipe my nose.

Nothing to amaze, nothing to astound,
all of me is normal, just the other way round.
So, for example, as I always explain,
my bottom's the place where I keep my brain.

I'm downside-up, I'm Upside-Down.
What looks like a smile can be really a frown,
as sometimes I feel lonely and do start to wonder
if I might find an upside-down auntie Down Under.

For I'm the unique upside-down man
walking the world on my arms and hands.
Now if you're not sure if it's me on the street,
I'll be the one waving with both my feet!

David Horner

Mrs Rabarua

We never knew
What Mrs Rabarua
Was after
Fishing down the sewer,
Ever optimistic
She'd take off the manhole cover,
Drop down her bait
And wait.
And wait.
And wait.
"These days
There are fewer
Down the sewer,"
Sighed Mrs Rabarua.

Brian Patten

Don't Cry For Me,
Pickled Onion

I'm a pickled onion
In the gherkin jar
I don't know how I got here
It's most peculiar

I can't do much about it
Though it's most illogical
So I'll just grin and bear it
Be philosophical

I suppose that I could try to find
A vinegary disguise
But no, I'll wait, and just be me
And give someone a surprise.

Roger Stevens

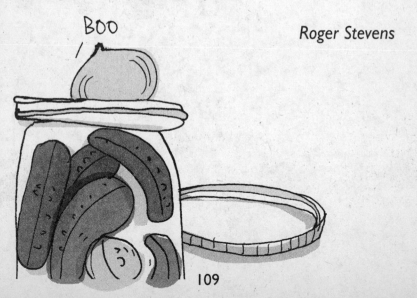

BOO

Caterpillar Salad Rap

caterpillar salad, butterfly flan
ants from the pantry boiled in a pan
bumble crumble, waspy jam
beetle treacle, fleas with ham
leech quiche, maggots-in-a-clam
lice in your rice like grains of sand
worm spaghetti on your hand
ladybird curd, that's the plan –
caterpillar salad, butterfly flan

Philip Burton

Good Luck! Or
Sound Advice from the Poet

(who spilt salt on to a black cat under a ladder
one Friday, and lived to tell the tale).

Never bake bread on a Sunday
If the wind is in the West,
Or stand on your head on a Monday
If you're wearing a long-sleeved vest.

If you meet with a ginger-bearded man
You should pull your ears and sing,
Or say this rhyme as fast as you can,
Or dance the Highland Fling.

Never wear skates in swimming pools,
Quack when you pass a duck.
If you keep to all these simple rules,
You'll always have good luck.
        Good Luck!

Gerard Benson

How rude

Last Word

From Simple Questions

Is a sick bed
a bed
that is feeling unwell?

Is a crime wave
a criminal's
wave of farewell?

Is a bent copper
a policeman
who has gone round the bend?

Is the bottom line
the line
on your bottom? The End.

Roger McGough

Acknowledgements

The compiler and publishers would like to thank the following for permission to use copyright material in this collection. The publishers have made every effort to contact the copyright holders but there are a few cases where it has not been possible to do so. We would be grateful to hear from anyone who can enable us to contact them so that the omission can be corrected at the first opportunity.

David Bateman for "Flicking Off The Filthy Flecks".
Gerard Benson for "Good Luck! (Or Sound Advice from the Poet)" © Gerard Benson from *Omba Bolomba, Poems by Gerard Benson,* pub. Smith/Doorstop Books, 2005.
Matt Black for "The Shortest Riddle In The World".
Redvers Brandling for "Jumble Sale Offer".
Philip Burton for "Caterpillar Salad Rap".
James Carter for "Fizz" © James Carter from *Page to Stage,* pub. David Fulton, 2005.
Richard Caley for "There Was A Goalkeeper From Seoul".
Jane Clarke for "Itch Hiker".
John Coldwell for "Ten Rhyming Things That Should Not Be Eaten".
Paul Cookson for "Epitaph for the Last Martian", "Death of a Dog Burglar", "Naughty Acrostic", "An Alphabet of Alphabeastical Facts You Didn't Know You Knew", "Haiku or High Queue?", "First Lines of Long Lost Nursery Rhymes", "There Was A Young Poet From Limerick", "Octopuzzles" (with help from Class 8MR, North Kesteven School), and "Frack to Bont".
Sue Cowling for "Limerick".
Ian Corns for "What's In My Basket?".

Karen Costello-McFeat for "Assassination".

Brian G D'Arcy for "Fame".

Graham Denton for "Men in Tights" © Graham Denton from *You're Not Going Out Like That!*, pub. Macmillan, 2003.

Peter Dixon for "King Harold" and "Jack".

Dorling Kindersley for "Fred" by Barry Buckingham first published in *Funfax: Limericks,* pub. © Henderson Publishing, 1996.

Gina Douthwaite for "Wigwise" © Gina Douthwaite from *Kersplosh, Kersplash, Kersplat*, pub. Oxford University Press, 2001.

Richard Edwards for "H. Houdini".

Eric Finney for "Four Soccer Clerihews", "The Year in Limericks" and "Sore Sorcerer".

John Foster for "A Batty Booklist", "Rapping Haiku" and "Animal Antics".

David Harmer for "Riddle Me Wrong", "Ten Tasty Snacks That Didn't Catch On" and "Why You Should Never Play On Roads".

Trevor Harvey for "A Slimline Grave", "Mapping It Out" and "Please Don't Believe A Word".

Stuart Henderson for "Spud-u-will-not-like".

Tim Hopkins for "Three Little Dogs".

David Horner for "New Rhymes for Old" © David Horner *Literacy and Learning* magazine, 1997, "Uncle Upside-Down" © David Horner from *Big Deal,* pub. Apple Pie, 2002 and "Epitaph".

Mike Johnson for "Science Lesson" © Mike Johnson from *Ridiculous Rhymes* ed. John Foster, pub. Collins, 2001, and "Told You So".

Clare Kirwan for "Flu Haiku".

David Kitchen for "Battling Natalie".

Trevor Dickinson for "Hurly-Burly Early Rhymes".

Ian Larmont for "Shirley Smithson (The Stunning Supermarket Shelf Stacker)" and "False Teeth".

Daniel Lawrence Phelps for "A Grave Mistake".

Rupert M Loydell for "Found Animal Rights Poem".

Roger McGough for extract from "Simple Questions" © Roger McGough from *All the Best,* pub. Puffin, 2003.

Trevor Millum for "That Dreadful Pupil From Leicester".

Spike Milligan for "Nonsense II" © Spike Milligan Productions Ltd, 1999, from *A Children's Treasury of Milligan,* Virgin Publishing Ltd.

Brian Moses for "Never Seen…".

Judith Nicholls for "Explosive Tale" © Judith Nicholls, from *Shadow Rap,* pub. Hodder Murray, 2005 and "The Cautionary Tale of Annabel Thaw".

Trevor Parsons for "Animal Quiz (v. difficult)" and "IQ Haiku".

Brian Patten for "Mrs Rabarua".

Eric Petrie for "What a Way to Go!".

Michael Rosen for "Nursery" © Michael Rosen from *DON'T Put Mustard in the Custard,* pub. André Deutsch, 1985.

Robert Scotellaro for "All in a Knight's Work".

Andy Seed for "Easy Mistake to Make".

Andrea Shavick for "Peter Pan".

Celia Stanzas for "Warning" and "Nutty Nonsense".

Roger Stevens for "Dogs' Swear Words", "Hey Diddle Diddle", "Peter Piper (Easy Version)", "Agnostic Shrimp" and "Don't Cry for Me, Pickled Onion".

Edward Stones for "Terrible Tombstones".

Nick Toczek for "The Total Flop".

Jill Townsend for "Superman" © Jill Townsend from *The Unidentified Frying Omelette,* pub. Hodder Wayland, 2000.

Philip Waddell for "Fighting Fit" and "Christmas Party Invitation List".

Clive Webster for "Riddle-me-ree" and "Twong Tister".

Look out for more fantastic poetry
collections from Scholastic...

Family
Poems

compiled by
Jennifer
Curry

Poems

SCHOLASTIC

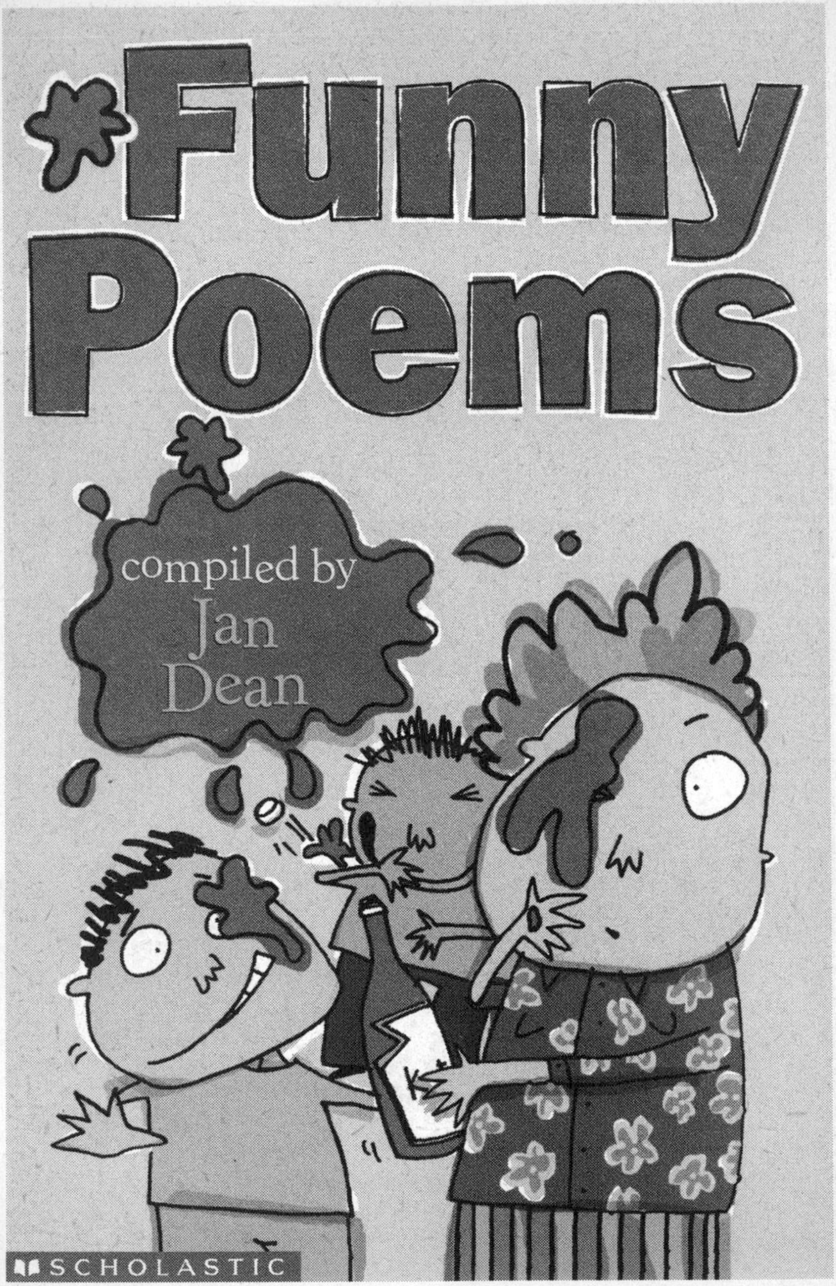

Funny Poems
compiled by Jan Dean
SCHOLASTIC

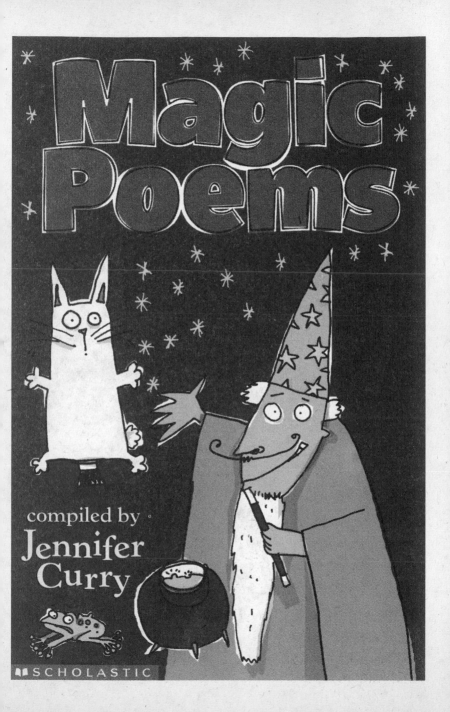

Pet Poems

compiled by
Jennifer
Curry

SCHOLASTIC

School
Poems

compiled
by
Jennifer
Curry

SCHOLASTIC

Spooky Poems

compiled by Jennifer Curry

SCHOLASTIC